The Turtle Tank

To Timothy, with love from Aunt Tina

Other Schiffer Books By The Author:
The Fish Tank, 978-0-7643-3706-2, $16.99
The Rat Tank, 978-0-7643-3842-7, $16.99

Type set in Taffy and Edwardian Script

ISBN: 978-0-7643-3843-4
Printed in China

Schiffer Books are available at special discounts for bulk purchases for sales promotions or premiums. Special editions, including personalized covers, corporate imprints, and excerpts can be created in large quantities for special needs. For more information contact the publisher:

Published by Schiffer Publishing Ltd.
4880 Lower Valley Road
Atglen, PA 19310
Phone: (610) 593-1777; Fax: (610) 593-2002
E-mail: Info@schifferbooks.com

For the largest selection of fine reference books on this and related subjects, please visit our website at www.schifferbooks.com
We are always looking for people to write books on new and related subjects. If you have an idea for a book please contact us at the above address.

This book may be purchased from the publisher.
Include $5.00 for shipping.
Please try your bookstore first.
You may write for a free catalog.
In Europe, Schiffer books are distributed by
Bushwood Books
6 Marksbury Ave.
Kew Gardens
Surrey TW9 4JF England
Phone: 44 (0) 20 8392 8585; Fax: 44 (0) 20 8392 9876
E-mail: info@bushwoodbooks.co.uk
Website: www.bushwoodbooks.co.uk

The Turtle Tank

Kristina Henry

Illustration by Laura Ambler and Amanda Brown

Schiffer Publishing Ltd®

4880 Lower Valley Road Atglen, Pennsylvania 19310

Turtles share a tank.
While one likes outside, other
Prefers the inside.

There it is! The big
Hand. Shy turtle quickly hides
In shell till hand goes.

All is clear. Turtle
Paddles over to his friend,
Who welcomes the hand.

Fingers grab hold. Lift.
Take friend to the outside world.
One is left behind.

He is so lonely.
What is out there? Beyond tank?
It's a mystery.

Shell works like a house.
To protect what's inside. So,
Turtle stays within.

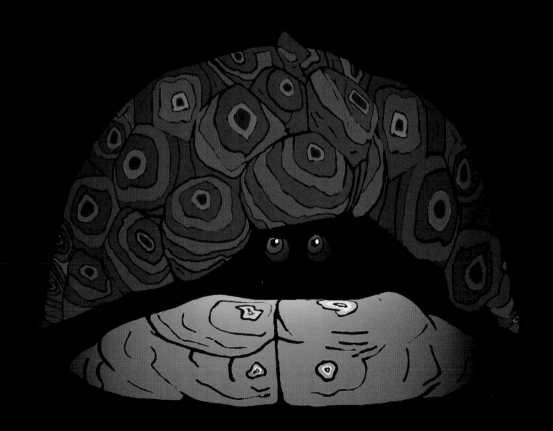

When he is hungry,
He will eat at night. Except
Friend eats during day.

Friend is returned to
The tank. He is warm and pleased.
Friend bobs head. *Try it.*

No thank you. I'll stay.
But suddenly he's lifted.
Uh oh! What is this?

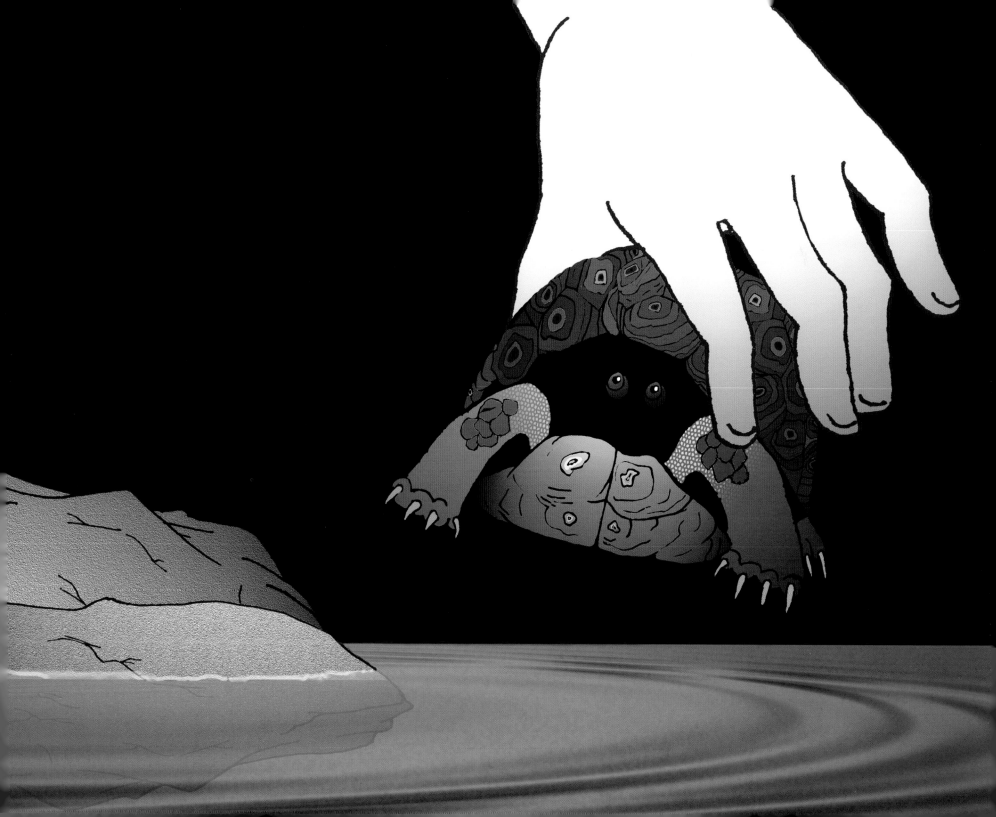

Below is warm, soft.
But turtle waits until all
Is still. Then he moves.

Bit by bit he pokes
His head out. It's a meadow!
Turtle looks both ways.

He stretches his legs,
And munches a flower. Yum!
Decides to advance.

Sun makes him feel warm.
Time goes by. Turtle floats up.
But keeps his head out.

Returns to his tank.
He misses his friend and log.
Water feels so good.

Tomorrow they can
Go together. Two turtles
Outside in the sun.

Walking in a field,
With lots of flowers to eat.
Both worlds are so nice.

About the Author

Kristina Henry grew up in Vienna, Virginia. She was graduated from Washington College in Chestertown, Maryland in 1988. Henry has worked as a technical writer, public relations director and substitute teacher. Her work has appeared in The Washington Post, USA Today, and The Washingtonian magazine. She is the author of the books, *The Fish Tank, The Rat Tank,* and *The Turtle Tank,* as well as *Sam: The Tale Of A Chesapeake Bay Rockfish.* She lives in Easton, Maryland, with her husband Mike.

About the Illustrators

Laura Ambler is proof that you don't need to leave home to reinvent yourself. The former Telly Award-winning advertising executive was bored in her industry and looking for something new to stir her creative juices. In Insert image 1998 she enrolled in a screenwriting class offered at Johns Hopkins University and a year later had launched a career in Hollywood—without ever leaving her hometown of Easton, Maryland.

Ambler is a member of the Writer's Guild of America East and has written approximately twenty screenplays, including *The White Pony,* produced by legendary producer and director, Roger Corman. She also wrote and produced the children's videos *Horses A to Z, Airplanes A to Z,* and *I Love Horses.*

Amanda Brown was born and raised on the Eastern Shore of Maryland. Her illustrations have appeared in *The Fish Tank, The Turtle Tank,* and *The Rat Tank.* She currently lives with two crazy kittens, Zero and Yukki, in Easton, Maryland, where she attends a local college. In her spare time, Amanda enjoys cooking, sewing, and drawing comics about her friends.